Just a Soldier

A story of one soldier's experience
as a German POW during WW II

by

Karyn Finneron

With illustrations by Dan Feeley

ISBN 978-0-9857362-3-1

First edition 2016

Printed in the United States of America

Thank you for supporting a self-published author!

To order additional copies of Just a Soldier, contact:

Karyn Finneron
Massachusetts USA
http://nanas-stories.com/

Don't forget to mention how you would like the author to personally autograph your book!

DEDICATION

This book is dedicated to my father-in-law, John Francis Finneron and to the countless number of United States and Allied Service men and women who fought and died for freedom for their countries and for the their generation and the ones that have followed. Never let us ever forget them and their sacrifice.

I. HISTORY REPEATS ITSELF

World War I was to be "the war to end all wars", or so we were told. Sometimes, we humans are a tough bunch, especially when it comes to learning a lesson. The world at large was reeling from the effects of World War I. As Americans, the feeling was that as things moved forward, Europe should be able to take care of itself and United States would take care of its issues. There was a strong feeling of isolationism in the country. This is not to say that our allies in Europe were not without assistance from the United States. Our country helped with the post war effort by providing supplies and money to rebuild the damage caused by the Triple Alliance, (Austria/Hungary, Germany and Italy).

In 1919 at a Paris peace conference, the leaders from the Allied governments, met to draft the treaty that was to make note of the official ending of World War I. All of the Allied governments were represented but the decisions were primarily made by England, France and the United States. The Allies blamed Germany for the war and, they wanted them to be severely punished. The agreement was named the Treaty of Versailles. This treaty severely carved up the lands that were known as the German and Austro-Hungarian Empire. The representatives from the German delegation were shocked by the severity of the document. They felt that this was not what they had originally agreed to during the surrender agreement made at the end of World War I. Essentially all of the blame for the war was placed on Germany.

Also, at this time, President Wilson introduced the League of Nations to try and prevent any future wars. This organization was to include all nations of the world who would, in times of disagreement and conflict, come together and discuss how to resolve their conflicts and ultimately prevent war. This organization would have been similar to what we call the United Nations today. Unfortunately, when President Wilson brought the idea back home, and presented it for a vote, the U.S. Senate did not ratify it. As a result the United States and Russia opted out. So, at this point in history, the idea of a League of Nations, was not to be because without United States and Russia, two of the most powerful nations in the world; it would probably fail. As a result of the decisions made at the Paris peace conference, Hitler would later cite the unfairness of the Treaty of Versailles as an example of how unfair the Allies had treated the Germans. This example, along with Hitler's fiery and passionate speeches, did much to rally his country and the military on his way to power.

As the world was recovering from World War I, and after losing the battle to form a League of Nations, President Wilson got back to the job of governing the country. Fortunately for the United States, the physical destruction of the war faced by the European nations had little if any effect on us. The 1920's brought a sense of prosperity to the United States. There was an attitude among the people in the U.S. that we had saved the world from the Axis powers and, moved the world forward toward democracy. The 1920's also proved to be a time of great social and economic upheaval.

In 1922, in Italy, Benito Mussolini was taking power. His political stance leaned toward Fascism. This meant that the government was in control of all means of production; as a result the bulk of the workers became government employees under this regime. To a degree this movement helped Italy to get back on its feet after the war. However, history would prove within a short time that Mussolini was not to be the savior of his country. In the not too distant future, he would form an alliance with Adolf Hitler, as the world once again began plummeting into another war.

In the early 1930's, a virtually unknown Adolf Hitler, began his rise to power by starting the Nazi Party, (National Socialist German Worker's Party). In 1932 many German voters became so impressed with Hitler's promises that the Nazi Party held the majority of seats in the Reichstag, the German Parliament. In January of 1933, Germany's president appointed Adolf Hitler as the chancellor of Germany. In March of the same year the Reichstag passed a law allowing the Chancellor, Hitler's government, to by-pass the German constitution and make laws without seeking the approval of the Reichstag and the German President. Hitler had now become a dictator, a leader who was granted absolute power.

Hitler was on the march in his mind and in his person. He wasted no time in moving forward his ideas to restore Germany to power. He developed a special police force made up of Nazi extremists and soon put them to work to secure his ambitions. This special police force was known as the SS or *Schutzstaffel*, which translated to "Protective Echelon." This special force initially served as Hitler's bodyguard. The SS were to become the most feared organization in all of Germany. They were responsible for the intelligence sector of the German army and were used as the forces and guards who ran the German concentration camps. After the war, the organization was deemed to be a criminal organization. Any and all captured SS members were tried as war criminals.

Hitler soon disbanded all the trade unions and outlawed all political parties with the exception of the Nazi Party. Soon the special police force, under Hitler's command was arresting anyone considered to be undesirable or threatening to the new government. The undesirables included Jews, Gypsies, intellectuals, the handicapped, priests and anyone considered to be "different" according to Nazi standards. Once anyone was arrested, little could be done for them, as they were given an unfair trial. After the trial they were shipped off to prison camps where they were tortured and killed. In 1934, President Hindenburg died and Hitler named himself the new president of Germany. His new regime was named the Third Reich or third empire. At this time he secretly told his generals to prepare for war.

In addition to organizing a military and a special police force Hitler had also begun to make it mandatory for all young people to join the Nazi Youth Movement. The organization had started in 1922 with a purpose of raising young people to be totally devoted to Germany, Hitler and the Nazi party. Meetings were held and young people were indoctrinated with various propaganda ideas of the Nazi party. The meetings involved physical activities including athletics, hiking and other physical fitness activities that were meant to prepare future generations for the work needed to protect Germany and, keep it as the leader of the world. Films were shown high lighting the cruelty of the Allies. They demonstrated how unfairly Germany was treated by the Treaty of Versailles and, of course how vile the Jewish people and "undesirables" were for the country. In 1936, it was mandated that all German youth join the movement.

In 1935 Hitler took a bold step in publically declaring that he was rebelling against the Treaty of Versailles. He had already been employing German engineers to design and build new and powerful tanks, submarines and weapons. He also announced the development of a German air force called the *Luftwaffe* and called for the recruitment of thousands of men for the German army. The plan also called for the expansion of the German navy. By 1939, the German armed forces had reached 4.5 million troops.

One year later, in direct opposition to the treaty, he ordered troops to the Rhineland. This area of Germany borders France, Belgium and the Netherlands. Although the treaty specifically stated that the German military was subject to force if it entered the Rhineland, Hitler proceeded to march forward. In addition, he had sent troops into Austria to take over that country. Though many Austrians were in favor of the unification of the two countries because many Austrians were of German descent, including Hitler himself; this was also in opposition to the treaty set after World War I. So as the German forces marched, the world looked on and did nothing to stop the advance.

As Hitler's army started its march, the German government stripped those labeled Jews of their citizen ship. Marriage between Germans and Jews was forbidden, Jews could no longer work for the government or in universities and all Jewish businesses were boycotted. The Jewish people of Germany and Austria were being gathered up and forced into small cramped areas of the cities called ghettos.

After being so successful in Austria and Germany, Hitler set his sights on Czechoslovakia. The Czechs did not want to let part of their country go without a fight. In hopes of protecting and keeping their country intact, they called on other European countries to help them convince Hitler to stop his advance. Hitler vowed to take the country by force if they did not hand over the portion of the country he wanted. This portion of Czechoslovakia was known as the *Sudetenland.*

Representatives of Germany, Britain, France and Italy met in Munich. Germany was attempting to settle the manner. Czechoslovakia was left out of the discussion that would eventually seal its' fate. In order to keep peace, the parties agreed to transfer Sudetenland to Germany providing Hitler would promise to settle future differences through meetings with representatives of nations rather than use war. Britain's Prime Minister, Neville Chamberlain stated after the meeting that the Munich Agreement represented "peace with honor." It took Hitler only five months to ignore the Munich Agreement and his troops invaded the rest of Czechoslovakia in order to claim it for the Reich.

On September 3, 1939, England and France declared war on Germany. This was done as a result of Hitler having seized Poland. As England declared war many of Britain's current and former colonies joined the effort as well. This brought Canada, Australia, India, South Africa and Rhodesia (now called Zimbabwe), into the war.

At this point the United States once again was trying to maintain the idea of isolation which was supported by many at home. As previously stated, the United States had recovered from World War I much more easily than Europe, because the war was not fought on U.S. soil. However, the U.S. was barely recuperating from the Great Depression when the war escalation in Europe began. Although the Allies were respected and the feelings toward helping our English friends were strong, no one was looking to jump into another war. The U.S. helped the European effort by sending food, munitions, clothes and economic aid to England. Germany was not about to let this effort continue and Germany's navy was put in action to sink the U.S. convoys on route to England.

In the early 1940's Germany, Japan and Italy joined forces to become the Axis Powers. Pearl Harbor in the Hawaiian Islands was surprised by an early Sunday morning bombing. Japan, on December 7, 1941, chose to send their air force to Pearl Harbor for the purpose of directly attacking the United

States. President Franklin D. Roosevelt in a radio address that was listened to across the country declared war on Japan. It was soon after Pearl Harbor that Germany declared war on the United States.

The story that follows is based on actual stories brought home by John Francis Finneron who fought in World War II. He also became a German prisoner after being captured during the Battle of the Bulge. The story is based in fact though the use of fiction has helped to round out the stories. John was just one soldier but we know there are many individual and collective stories of all the men and women from the Greatest Generation who served to help save the world for freedom. May their sacrifices never be forgotten.

2. PEACE TIME

Fitchburg, Massachusetts in the early 1940's would have definitely been described as small town America. It is located in the rolling hills of north, central Worcester County. There was always a strong French Canadian, Irish and Italian population along with Finns, Greeks and good old Yankees. It was a town that provided opportunities to work in the paper mills and various factories. Fitchburg had its own hospital as well as a thriving main street. It was a place to bring up a family, work hard and attend church on Sundays. There were good public schools and many parochial schools attached to the churches of the various ethnic groups that had settled there.

It was in this environment that John grew up. He was the oldest of eleven children. He was of Irish and French Canadian descent. His family belonged to the mostly Irish parish, known as St. Bernard. He and all of his siblings also attended St. Bernard's elementary and later high school. Being the oldest, John learned early on what responsibility was, and the importance of helping his father and mother with the rest of the children. His mom and dad had done a good job raising the family during the Great Depression. The fact that the children continued with school during this time was no easy feat and a wonderful testimony to the value his family placed on education. During one tough period in the Finneron family, John dropped out of high school for a year to help out with the finances. After a year his parents advised him to go back and finish his last year of high school. That was where he met his sweetheart, Mary Margaret Darcy. He always felt it was a good thing he went back to school, for many reasons, but mostly because of Mary.

The U.S. was finally coming out of the Great Depression. John had a decent job at Schulties Smoke shop on Main Street. He and Mary married in September of 1941, and life in general was quite good but life and circumstances were about to change that.

Recently, the U.S. was all abuzz about the escalating war that was going on in Europe. The country was trying hard to stay out of the war. The feeling in the country politically was one of isolationism. They did not want to be dragged into a war that was focused on Europe's issues with Germany and the rise to power of Adolf Hitler. The U.S. promised it would help England and the allied forces by sending ships filled with supplies, munitions and food, anything that would help their friends in England.

Europe had been at war from some time now and Germany's leader, Adolf Hitler was using his army to march across Europe and take over any country in their path. Germany had formed an alliance with Italy and Japan which became known as the Axis Powers. In Germany itself, many people, but especially the Jews had been forced into the ghettos or rounded up and sent off to concentration camps. By now, Hitler as "*der Fuhrer*" (the leader), of the German military had his eyes set on taking over the world and bringing Germany back to the status it held before World War I.

England, in the past had been somewhat protected and safe from outside invasion. As an island nation, they had most always been in a position to protect and defend their country as well as themselves from various invaders. But, this was the twentieth century with planes, battleships and submarines. All methods of transportation had greatly improved over the years following World War I so, no country could be considered to be safe, from any type of invasion. England had been asking the U.S. to join them in the fight but President Roosevelt was trying to keep his country out of war.

So many newspaper articles and broadcasts on the radio were filled with horrible stories of death and destruction and although there was a small hope that the U.S. would not get into the war, many were feeling that it would eventually happen.

In 1940, John had registered for the draft, which was required for all men eighteen and over. Life in general was going on in the same fashion it had for several years in Fitchburg. John got up every day and walked to his job at the smoke shop. His job was an enjoyable one but, what John liked most of all was meeting all the different people who came into the store. There were neighbors, friends even business men from out of town. Of course now almost everyone that came in was only interested in what might happen with the war. Would Europe manage alone? Would the U.S. get involved in order to help their English and French Allies? Everyone had questions but not many answers.

In addition to worrying about what might happen if war broke out; he was also wondering what Mary would do if he was off fighting in some foreign place. Of course he would go, that was what you did when you became a man; take care of your family and take care of your country, if you were needed. He hoped and prayed that his country would not get into the war. He also hoped if it did, he would not get called. John knew if that happened, he would be there for his country.

The U.S. soon found they did not have to worry about the war with Europe, because on December 7, 1941, Pearl Harbor in the U.S. territory of Hawaii, was bombed in a surprise attack by Japan. That was the beginning, officially of World War II for the United States. Many lives were lost, most of the United States' fleet in the Pacific was destroyed and the country was in shock. President Roosevelt came on the radio and spoke to the country. Everyone on that day, including John and Mary, were glued to the radio. The president spoke saying that this attack on this day "…would live in infamy…." President Roosevelt also stressed that the country was facing "... grave danger…" because of the surprise attack. He really rallied the country around this terrible tragedy and time in our history. Soon men were enlisting in all branches of the service, being drafted into the army and preparing for what was to be a devastating time in the history of the world.

3. WAR TIME

As many young men flocked to enlist in the armed services, John did not enlist. If he got drafted he would go, but Mary had just told him that she might be expecting their first baby. John felt that he should at least wait for the call to be drafted and take it from there. There was no doubt, that if his country needed him, he would go. He was registered for the draft and if his country wanted him, they knew how to contact him. The decision was made to wait and see.

Several weeks went by and Mary went to the doctor and came home with the wonderful news that she was in fact expecting a baby and she was due in October. The war for the U.S. had now been going on several months. Battles were continuing in Europe against Hitler and the Nazis. Allied Forces were also engaged in battle with Mussolini and the Italian forces in Sicily and Africa. There was also heavy fighting going on in the Pacific with Japan. Germany, Italy and Japan were now allies that were united against the rest of the world.

John still did not receive his draft notice. Each day was so stressful with worrying about whether or not the mail would bring the letter they all knew would eventually come. Checking the mail box every day for the draft notice was filled with anxiety for Mary as well as John. Each week that went by also meant that Mary was one week closer to delivering the baby.

All they could do was to wait and see, hope and pray that the letter would come after the baby was born.

The months flew bye and eventually John's letter came requiring him to report to the draft board for induction into the army. John and Mary just hugged each other and hoped for the best. The greatest concern was that there were several weeks left to wait before the baby was due. John advised Mary that they had been so lucky so far and with faith and hope they would all get through this difficult time.

On the day that John was to report to the draft board he had an idea. He was going to ask if he could be deferred until the baby was born. He knew he was asking a lot but it couldn't hurt. The worst they could do was to deny the request. He did not tell Mary his plan because, he didn't want to worry her or get her hopes up, but he would give it a try.

When John had his physical exam to determine if he was fit to fight, he found that he was drafted for limited service because his eyes were so bad, even with his prescription glasses. This was not the news he wanted to hear and, he didn't know what that would really mean once he was actually in the service. It did not change his mind though, he still would ask about the deferment. John soon discovered that there were a number of men asking for deferments, the reasons were also many. It seemed like the chances were slim that his request would be granted but John decided on faith and hope to get him through.

John asked the draft board about the possibility of waiting for Mary to have the baby. After much discussion the board granted his request and told him to report back to them when the baby was born. John was so grateful. He thanked the board and ran home to tell Mary the news.

As soon as he arrived home, he went right to Mary, and told her about his limited duty status. He also told her that he had asked the draft board if he could be deferred, just until the baby arrived. Mary just smiled and hugged John when he told her the request had been granted. A few days later the official letter came stating that John was deferred. The letter stated that he must report back to the board once the baby was born. They both breathed a sigh of relief and now looked forward to preparing for their new baby.

On October 20, 1942, Mary woke up and told John she felt it was time for the baby to come and they needed to get to the hospital. Off they went and soon after had a beautiful baby girl that they named Joan. That morning, as soon as John was sure that the baby and Mary were fine, he took a taxi to the draft board. He went into the draft board office and reported that his baby was born. "I am ready to go as promised." John told the same judge that had granted the deferment. The judge at the court house could not believe that he came the very day the baby was born. He just looked at John and said "Son don't worry. You will be getting a letter stating when to report. Go and be with your wife and baby." John left the draft board feeling so happy and blessed. He had a beautiful new baby, a wonderful wife but, he also felt a great sense of responsibility to his country because; they had allowed him the privilege of being with Mary until the baby was born. He knew it was now time to do his duty.

4. "YOU'RE IN THE ARMY NOW"

The next few weeks flew bye and on July 8, 1943, John entered the service. He went from Fitchburg, Massachusetts to Fort Devens in Ayer, Massachusetts for basic training. After completing basic training John was on to Fort Eustis, Virginia for anti-air craft training. He had never been so far from home. The furthest he had ever been was to New York City on his honeymoon and he had Mary with him. He was homesick but at least for now he was in the states and he knew Mary and the baby would be fine because of all the close family in Fitchburg.

In the first several months of military service, John saw a lot more of the country that he had ever imagined. He was transferred to Texas, California, Colorado and Maryland. In Texas he became part of the ground crew that supported the Air Force. All of the transfers were for various training that would be needed if and when he got to go overseas. Because of his "limited service" designation, he kept getting pushed back and was not ordered to go overseas. John said "good bye" to many of his friends that had trained with him. Each time a group went without John, he had to get used to a new group and make new friends. The longer he was in the states he felt safe but each day that went by John knew the odds were he would be going overseas. It was a waiting game that often weighed heavy on his mind. Finally, one day he went to his commanding officer and told him it was difficult to see the guys he served with being shipped out while he had to stay behind. The commanding officer advised John that he would most likely be going soon. John asked if there was any way he could go out with the next group that would be going overseas. His commanding officer said he would see what he could do about the situation but his "limited service" status was not helping the issue. John hoped and prayed that if and when he went it would be with the guys he knew best. He knew having buddies who had your back when things got tough would be very helpful.

The orders came in August of 1944, John and his fellow soldiers were to be shipped out. There was to be a short leave at home and then they would all report back to be shipped overseas. The leave at home was bittersweet. It was great to see Mary and baby Joan but the thought of leaving to go to war hung over them. The day to report back for duty arrived so quickly and with hugs and kisses and promises to write and pray for John, he was off to war.

Once back on base all of John's fellow soldiers being shipped out were running a wave of emotion. You could see fear, excitement, anxiety and even humor in so many of the faces of his comrades. No one really knew what to expect and even if they did some of them would never believe what war was actually like. They were off to England and then would go on to the front lines. John's group was following the D Day invasion which had been biggest amphibious assault in history. A lot of lives had been lost and the Allies had suffered greatly. However, D Day also became the turning point in the war for the Allies. Although this was the turning point, there would still be a lot of fighting to do. France had also been liberated in 1944 and the Germans had been pushed back but they were not defeated.

John was assigned to the second division of the 38th regiment and for six long months the Allied forces kept hammering at the German lines. The hope was to cause as much damage as possible and to weaken any further German offensive.

When he wasn't working at being a good soldier, he thought a lot about Mary and the baby. He spent a lot of time praying that he would get back to them in one piece. He was so glad to have his strong Catholic upbringing which gave him the faith to hope and believe he would get back home. He kept a cross around his neck along with his dog tags and whenever there was a minute he prayed, for himself and for all the soldiers that were fighting in this awful war. He wrote home as often as he could and tried to make his letters sound happy so Mary would not worry too much but, it was a hard job. He was so lonely at times and if he was being really honest; he would say he was more afraid than he had ever been in his life. Hard work and preparation for battle kept his mind occupied during the days but the nights could be difficult. In addition, the December winter weather had descended upon them and there was never a day when the cold didn't bother everyone. It felt like they would never be warm again.

Lately a lot of fellow soldiers had been talking about the rumors they had heard. It seemed as if there was going to be another potentially large Allied offensive. The rumors seemed to be focused on battle plans very near to where the 38th was at the time. His unit was in the Ardennes section of Belgium very near Bastogne. Everyone was saying this was going to be a huge offensive meant to finally push the Germans towards surrender. There certainly had been lots of skirmishes all around them and a day never went by without the sound of guns and shells all around them. John and his fellow soldiers just kept hoping and praying whatever it was would happen soon and the war would be coming to a close.

On December 15, there was news of the German Army moving men and equipment across one of the nearby rivers. All of this movement was extremely close to the Allies and their garrisons. This was it! This was to be the beginning of the big offensive that John and all his buddies had been hearing about. Little did John and his buddies know at the time, but the Battle of the Bulge, as this offensive was called; was going to go down in history as one of the major battles of the war. It would also be a real turning point for the Allies as well as the beginning of the demise of the Germans. Right now all they were concerned with was, "when would it all begin?" How would it all go and would they, by the grace of God, all get back home in one piece and alive?

5. The Bulge

Every day now there were on going skirmishes with the enemy. The soldiers would hear on one day that they were making a difference in pushing back the Germans; only to hear the next day that the Allies were being pushed back. There was confusion and havoc at times on every front. The Germans were trying desperately to break through the Allies in order to capture their fuel depot. The Germans were in desperate need for fuel for their military vehicles.

The battle had begun and was so fierce, there were German troops everywhere. The allied soldiers were suffering heavy casualties. To make matters worse the miserable December weather with storms, freezing temperatures were not helping the cause at all. John's unit commander decided the best thing was to split up and try to "stay under the radar" and try to get back to the main unit of the army. John saw a church close by and thought "if I can get to the church maybe I can stay alive long enough to get by the Germans once it is dark, and get back to my guys." John ran, he made it to the church, hugged the walls and stayed below the windows. No sooner did he get inside when he heard German soldiers outside the church. He was hoping he would be safe until they passed by and then he would make a break to get back to his unit. John could hear them passing by several times but lucky for him they did not enter the church. He didn't know if it was his prayers or sheer luck but whatever it was, John made it out of the church and started on the painful journey to find his way back to the main branch of the Allied forces. He slept little and hid as best he could. After walking for what seemed like a very long time he came upon an empty warehouse. He decided to go inside and hide for a bit while he tried to warm up and get his bearings before moving on toward the allies and his unit. Unfortunately for John his luck was about to run out.

John did not realize that while he was running for the shelter of the warehouse, he had been seen by several German troops. All of a sudden he heard what he knew was a grenade but he never saw it coming. The grenade that hit him was a known as concussion grenade. These grenades were designed to injure by concussion rather than by exploding and causing death. This type of grenade also allowed the soldier who was throwing the grenade to not have to take cover from his own weapon.

John was not only wounded by the concussion but, he also sustained a badly wounded hand. John awoke to find him and several other Allied troops captured. John knew being captured could be worse than being killed but, when you manage to stay alive, you still have a chance to be free. For now he would cling to that hope. The captured soldiers were on the march with several German soldiers guarding them. Soon they would be on a train that would bring them to a POW camp somewhere in Germany. John and his fellow prisoners were unaware at the time but the Battle of the Bulge would result in over 20,000 troops killed, over 42,000 wounded and over 21,000 captured. It was December 16, 1944. A day he would never forget.

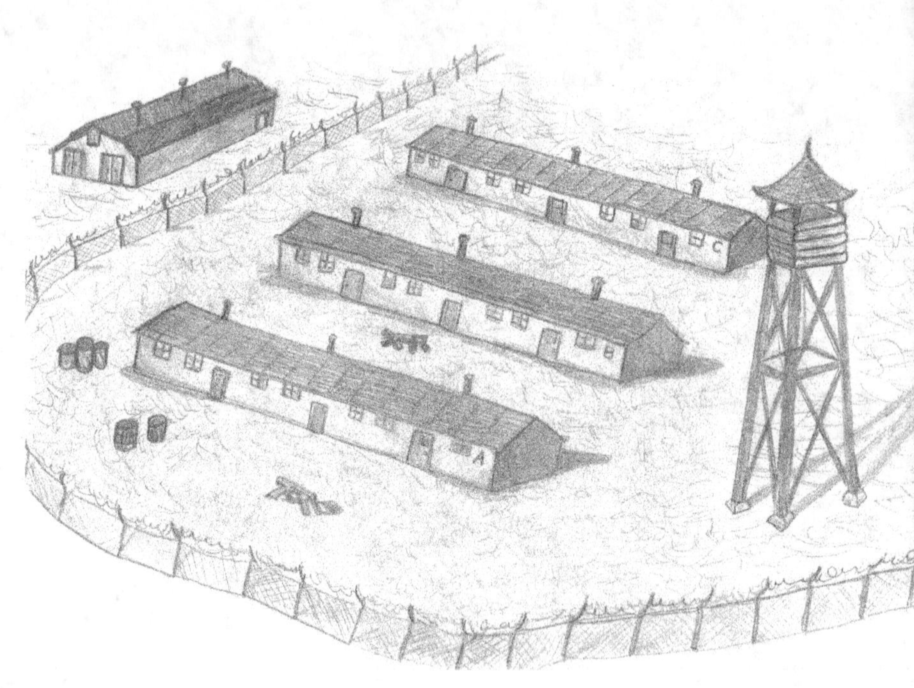

6. P.O.W.

John soon found out he was not the only prisoner. He was part of a larger group that had all been trying to get back to the main Allies' line but, like him they had never made it. There were about 100 American soldiers taken prisoner at that time. They were marched for a very long time and soon put on a train headed for Germany and Stalag IV B, one of the largest German prisoner of war camps of World War II. There was almost no talking on that train but a lot of scared and anxious faces as all of the soldiers wondered what would become of them. None of the guards on the train spoke to any of the prisoners. They were offered no food or water. The prisoners had no one to care for their wounds and some of them were pretty bad off and moaning in pain. To make matters worse there was no heat in the box car and they were crowded in the car like cattle. Everyone huddled together for warmth and tried to quietly console each other. As for John, he just closed his eyes and thanked God he was alive. He was hurt and shook up from the concussion grenade but he was alive. His next thoughts were for Mary and baby Joan. What would Mary do when she heard of his fate? How he wished he could spare her the worry but all he could do now was try and stay alive. Exhausted and with nothing else to do, he fell asleep.

Back home, Mary was busy working as a lot of women did

while their husbands and sweethearts were off to war. Mary considered herself lucky because she had family that could take care of Joan while she worked. She wrote to John everyday but was often not sure if the letters got through to where he was fighting. She tried to keep the letters light and happy but her heart was often heavy with worry. Lately she was very concerned because she had not heard from John since before Christmas. All the newspapers were filled with the huge battles being fought in Europe and in the Pacific. There wasn't anyone she knew who didn't have some male loved one off on some battlefield or warship. She and John even had brothers and cousins all over the world fighting this awful war. She prayed that the reason she hadn't heard from John was because there was no time to write and no way to get the mail home. The holidays had passed and so far it hadn't been much of a happy new year.

Soon the letters Mary had been sending John started to be returned. The letters were stamped either "MIA", (missing in action) or "Deceased." Now Mary had real cause for concern. She didn't understand because usually families had a visit from the armed forces telling them that their loved one had been killed or they received an official letter. To date, Mary had not had anything like that happen to her. With no official word about John and no letters she prayed and clung to the hope that he was alive somewhere. The night time was the worse, she hardly slept but she prayed and prayed. She poured over the newspapers every day looking for something that might give her some idea of where he could be. Maybe his regiment would be named as being involved in a battle, something, anything would help. Then, one day, a very official looking letter arrived from U.S. military's war department. Mary held her breath as she looked at the letter. It took a few moments to collect herself before opening it. The letter stated that John was missing and presumed dead as a result of the recent battle and engagement with the enemy on December 16, 1944. Mary refused to believe he was dead. She believed in her heart that she would know if he were dead and so she would not allow her faith to be shaken. The difficult task now was to go and tell John's mother that her oldest son was missing in action or possibly worse. It was a task that could not wait because Mary knew that soon the newspaper would have another announcement that one of Fitchburg's boys had met his demise.

When she arrived at her mother-in-law's home, she just got right to the task. She pulled out the letter and handed it to John's mother. "He's not dead." Mary said. "I won't believe it, not until they know for sure." Mary said, as she looked John's mother in the eye. John's mother just hugged her and said "we will hope and pray." Mary never cried; her faith was that strong. She left her mother-in-law's home and prayed all the way home; not just for John but for all the recently captured and killed.

The train ride that held the captured Allied soldiers seemed as if it would never end. It felt as if they were traveling at a snail's pace. Several of the prisoners were whispering about the rumors that had been circulating regarding the Germans attempt to capture the Allies fuel depot. They decided the slow pace must have been due to the Germans trying to conserve fuel. Suddenly the train came to a stop. Soon, a German soldier came into the car where they all were. "*ACHTUN*!" He yelled as he motioned for them to get up. Soon the door to the car was opened and the soldier was motioning for them to get out of the car. It was freezing out there and as far as they could see there was nothing but snow and trees. One by one they all jumped out of the train and were being forced marched in the dark, toward the trees. John started to think they were going to shoot them all and their bodies would never be found or they were going to be left there to freeze and die. Neither one of these things were good options.

On the march toward the trees, the snow was very deep and the going was slow, but the guards kept trying to make the prisoners go faster. Once they reached the trees the German guards said "*herunterkommen*!" as they motioned for them to get down on the ground. The prisoners all looked at each other with very scared faces. What would happen to them? John thought to himself, "This is it! I'm sorry Mary." Then they all heard two loud blasts. Everyone hugged the frozen ground as they felt it shake from the blasts. Now the German soldiers were yelling "*Achtun, Schnell, Schnell*!" as he started moving them back to the train as quickly as possible. The train started to move again and they all ran and got on the train. Two cars including the one they had been riding in were blown to bits. They had been spared. Once back on the train the prisoners all started to whisper about the incident. Had the soldiers purposely saved their lives? Why, they must have been risking their own lives to get them back to the train? Surely they would have been shot if the commanding officer had seen that they had saved the enemy! One of the prisoners whispered to several of his comrades who were nearby that the cars must have been blown because of the lack of fuel. Now the prisoners had a new worry. If they ran out of fuel before they got to camp, what would the German guards do with them? Surely they would all die of exposure. The question of the night was "why were they saved?" It didn't matter they were alive and that meant they still had a chance to make it home. John and his comrades were clinging to that hope.

After several days on the train they finally arrived at *Stalag IV B*. It was a few days before Christmas and the only present right now was that John and his comrades were alive. But it has been said that "there are worse things than dying," and they would soon find out how true these words could be. When the prisoners were marched out of the train, the site before them looked like a winter wasteland. There was not much activity due to the harsh winter weather but the isolation and frozen picture did not give anyone any real hope.

The prisoners were marched to a barracks that was no more than a wooden shack with a cook stove at one end not giving off much heat. The barracks had triple bunks and some running water. Each prisoner, about twelve to a barracks was given a ration of coal and wood for heating and cooking. In order to use the toilet you had to go outside. There were holes in the ground to use but no privacy not even a door on the building. There were several windows covered with frost inside and out. They were not issued any blankets or anything to fight the bone chilling cold. Many of the POWs that they saw on that first day looked unhealthy and sick. The camp smelled of desperation and death. It was most certainly going to be a difficult and painful stay. About the only good thing that day was discovering that this camp, unlike many they had all heard about, was not manned by the SS but by regular German troops. The SS troops were the most feared soldiers in the world. They were known for their cruelty and harsh treatment of anyone who crossed their paths. They were well known for persecution of the Jewish people, people with developmental or physical impairment and allied captured troops. At least on this account John and his fellow prisoners could breathe a little easier.

It wasn't long before they were assigned a bunk and barracks and made aware of what the daily routine was to be like. There were prisoners from England, France, Russia, Canada and the U.S. There was role call in the morning, and time to eat and assignments for various work details. The German soldiers tried to force the prisoners to do work that involved trying to repair the German trucks and fix other equipment that was housed in the town near the camp. The Red Cross had managed to inform the soldiers that they did not have to do any work that would be considered helping the German war effort. The soldiers soon refused to work. As a result the German soldiers stopped feeding them. The diet was extremely poor to begin with but, taking everything away was really tough on the hungry, cold prisoners.

When the prisoners managed to get food the diet consisted of turnip, cabbage and potato soup. The soup consisted mostly of broth and not much else. On Christmas day, the prisoners were all given a large bowl of cabbage soup. John would later remember that it was the best meal he ever had in the prison camp. For right now it just filled your belly and was at least warm.

The soldiers soon found out that the guards diet was often the same as theirs. It seemed like a less cruel punishment for the prisoners. How or why would they feed them if they barely had enough to feed themselves? The war had dragged on for such a long time that there was not much left with regards to food supplies. In addition, being in the middle of winter did not help. At times the prisoners would hear of Red Cross trucks arriving and they hoped it was food. Occasionally it was but the rations were poor and more often the trucks were carrying clothing and other nonedible supplies. The soldiers thought so much about food that during the night before falling asleep everyone started telling each other what they would eat once they got home. You would know where certain guys were from just by listening to what they wanted to eat. “I can’t wait to git me some grits and gravy when I’m back home. My momma makes the best grits.” stated one fellow from Georgia. “Well, I’m gonna have the biggest stack of pancakes and maple syrup from our sugar maple trees,” said another GI from Vermont. “How about you John, what do you want to eat,” asked a soldier from New York. “Baked Beans?” “I just want to go to my mom’s house on a Saturday morning after work with Mary and the baby and have lunch. My mother would always make a big pot of stewed tomatoes and macaroni for all of us. I never thought I would miss that but it sure would feel like a feast right now," John answered. John fell asleep thinking how strange to be starving and thinking of food.

One morning a German soldier came into the barracks and shouted "Finneron, *herkommen*" as he motioned for him to come to him. John got up and went to the soldier as he motioned for him to go outside. A few of his fellow prisoners also got up to go to John but he shook his head and waved them away. John had no idea what this was about and his gut told him to be alert and ready for anything. Maybe there was a work detail or some other duty to perform. What could it be?

The German soldier marched John to a section of the camp that was a bit isolated from the barracks and he told him to "Sit down" in perfect English. "Where are you from?" he asked. "What?" John said, "Why?" The German soldier said "tell me." "I'm from Massachusetts." John replied. "Yes, yes, but where?" The soldier asked again. "Near Boston, Fitchburg, Massachusetts," John answered. John continued to ask him if he knew where that was. "Yes, Yes, it is between Leominster and Gardner. "

John and the German soldier continued to talk. He told the guard where he worked and, the guard knew exactly where Schulties was; he had even gone in the store and been waited on by John. He said that the moment he saw John he had a feeling that he knew him from somewhere. The guard explained that when the war broke out he came back to Germany to try and get his parents and sister out and bring them to the U.S. They were on their way to a ship to take them to the states and they were stopped. They were not allowed to leave. His parents and sister had to return to their home. He was then drafted into the German army because he was still a German citizen. During the war his parent's home had been bombed; his entire family was killed. John said how sorry he was for his loss. The guard told John he would try and see what little he might be able to do for him but it would be difficult at best. The guard then shook John's hand and hurried him back to the barracks because it would not be good for either of them to be seen talking together. He asked John not to disclose their conversation and John nodded "yes" to the guard and told him to not put himself at risk to help him.

Not everyone survived the winter. Pneumonia, typhus and malnutrition were the most common reasons for the death. Each loss was made more difficult by the thought of "who would be next." Those who survived the winter knew it was an amazing feat because even if they were not sick, they were all starving. Morale continued to be up and down. In the spring of 1945 the soldiers started hearing rumors that the Allied forces were getting closer. There were also rumored sightings of American bombers which kept everyone's hopes for an end to the war alive. Also, several times recently, the camp itself was bombed. The prisoners had no real way to protect themselves other than to huddle together and lie on the floor of the barracks. If the POWs tried to leave the barracks for a better shelter they were either shot at or had the guard dogs chase them back to the barracks. John had started kneeling by his bed and holding on to the crucifix around his neck and prayed out loud. After several incidents of bombing, their barracks had been spared. Now whenever planes were heard overhead or bombs started to drop, several other POWs huddled around John and prayed with him.

On an early April morning in 1945, all of the prisoners in the camp were roused. They were told to gather their things, they were being moved. Some of the prisoners began asking "moved, where, what's happening?" They were told they were being moved to another camp, closer to the Allied lines. Rumors now were being circulated daily that the war was nearly over. The prisoners from Stalag IV B were being transferred to Stalag

Lutt I, located in Barth, Germany. They were loaded into trucks and moved approximately 150 miles closer to the Allied lines. This Stalag had been used to imprison allied airmen and officers for most of the war. Now however, if rumors were to be believed, the Germans would soon be retreating and forced to surrender. They were so close to being liberated, the question was would they be able to hang on until Germany surrendered.

On May 7, 1945 the war ended. The German guards came to open the gates of the camp and told the prisoners the direction to go. They advised that they would soon find the Allies by walking west. The guards told them to start walking. The prisoners were unsure if this was a trick or not. After being imprisoned for six months or more many of the men could hardly walk. John was one of those men. When he entered the service in 1942 he weighed 160 pounds stripped down. He was nowhere near that weight now. Struggling to walk a fellow GI named Pancho who had not been in prison as long as John picked him up. "Come on buddy, we're getting outta here!" Pancho just smiled at John and he could see the gratitude on his face. The quote "no man left behind" never meant more to John that in that moment. He had doubts if he could make it if the trek back to the Allied lines was to be very long but at least now he had hope. In his heart and mind he was repeating "I'm coming home Mary, I'm coming home."

John would soon find out once he got medical attention that he weighed 98 pounds fully dressed. He was hospitalized as many of the POWs were. He spent time in an English hospital and never had he felt so blessed to have made it to safety. He truly was going to get home!

7. Coming Home

John spent about twelve weeks in the hospital. Finally the day had come to be discharged and to go home. In August of 1945, John was back at Fort Devens in Ayer, Massachusetts. He had started his military journey there and it was fitting that he would finish it there. He had come full circle. Now he needed to get back to Fitchburg and Mary and his little girl.

When John was hospitalized in England, he began writing to Mary. He told her he was safe now and not to worry. He said how much he missed her and Joan and how anxious he was to get back home to them. John couldn't give Mary a definite date but he knew he would be home soon.

When the letter arrived, Mary was so happy and excited. She shared the letter with everyone, even little Joan. Mary picked up Joan and said "Your Daddy's coming home, big girl!" Joan smiled and repeated "Daddy home." "That's right, pretty soon," Mary responded.

John managed to get released from Fort Devens a little early and he got a friend to drive him to Fitchburg about a half an hour away. When John arrived at his home, no one was there. He knew Mary went out with her girlfriends to a movie every week so; he walked down to the theater to surprise her. He saw Mary and her friends and didn't say a word. He wanted to see if they would notice him. At first no one seemed to notice but then one of Mary's friends let out a scream! "John, John, Mary, look John is here, he's here!!" They all ran to him but no one was faster than Mary. They held on tight to each other and Mary kept feeling his arms. She couldn't believe after all the months of worry and praying that her John was finally home. He was finally going to get to see Joan and they could begin to be a family again.

Joan was with Mary's sister Sheila that day and they began the walk home together. That walk was one of the longest walks the young couple had ever taken. Everyone they passed stopped the young couple and welcomed John home and told Mary how lucky she was to have him back. Mary knew better than anyone how true that was. Things could now start to get back to normal again. They could begin their plans for a normal life.

Within the next month the war with Japan also ended. It took an atom bomb, the first nuclear weapon, to be dropped on Hiroshima and later Nagasaki to bring Japan to its knees. On September 2, 1945 the war was finally over.

The war and being a prisoner had left John with wounds that would plague him, to a degree, the rest of his life. The physical problems were mostly damage caused to his stomach and digestive tract. The long period of starvation and poor nutrition coupled with severe weight loss took a long time to heal. It took even longer for him to gain back the weight he had lost. He was hospitalized several times and sent to Lake Placid, NY for two weeks of rest and recuperation. The spouses of the POWs were allowed to go on this rest and recuperation trip with them. John was so appreciative of this because he did not want to be without Mary for any reason. On discharge from the service and from medical treatment John received five weeks of pay from the military. He also received a purple heart for being wounded. John went back to his job the day after he was cleared from his active duty and had a health clearance.

He and Mary went on to have five more children. There were two girls and four boys. He never spoke much about the war to his children. He was typical of so many men in that generation. He was called by his country to do a job. He loved his family, his God and his country. When the call came he went because it was the right thing to do. There was a time in his later years when he went through a bit of a depression. The counselor he met with tried to get him to talk about the war and even then he would not say much. The counselor stated to John, that he must have a lot of anger towards the Germans for what he went through. John responded that the experiences he had as a prisoner were bad but he harbored no anger or resentment towards the German soldiers he encountered.

John went on to explain that at the time he was captured the prison guards were not much better off than the prisoners. He relayed the stories of how he was spared death because of ordinary German soldiers. His answer to the counsellor was that "they were like me, fighting for their country."

John remembered Pancho who carried him to safety and remembered many of the men he was imprisoned with as well as those who died of battle wounds or disease and starvation. He never remembered the name of the German soldier who was his prison guard and never saw him again. He wondered if he ever made it out of the war. He also wondered how he could have gone on, knowing his family that he tried to get out of Germany, had died in one of the many bombings in Germany. He hoped that he was happy somewhere.

It took a granddaughter, Breanna, a high school student, at the time of the fiftieth anniversary of World War II to get him to speak about the war. Breanna's class assignment was to interview a World War II veteran. She chose her grandfather, just a soldier, to interview. Breanna stated in her interview piece that John, her grandfather kept saying during the interview "I'm just glad I'm here to tell you about it." "John, thank you, so were we."

Epilogue

The story of John Finneron is true. He did fight in the Bulge. He was missing and presumed dead for a time. He did spend time in Stalag IV B and Stalag Lutt I. The story of being saved on the train is also true as is the story about the German soldier who took John out of the barracks and spoke to him about Fitchburg. When John was telling his granddaughter his story he was seventy nine years old. He was unable to remember the soldier's name at that time but he was forever grateful to him and the German soldiers who took them off the train on route to Germany. In 1998, the movie SAVING PRIVATE RYAN came out and John's wife Mary asked if he would like to see it. Although he was not in the "D" Day battle his response was that he "I do not need to see it. I lived enough of it." In 2002, Breanna's story and full report was published in the Fitchburg Sentinel's July 4th edition. At that time John's health was failing and he was a resident in a nursing home in Leominster, MA. John died in December of 2005. This story could not have been written without Breanna's wonderful story and research that she provided.

GLOSSARY

Amphibious – vehicles able to operate on both land and water

Axis Powers- Composed of Germany, Italy and Japan who formed an alliance against the Allied forces of World War II

D Day- The invasion of Normandy, France by Western Allied forces on June 6, 1944.

Dictator – ruler who wields absolute authority. A country ruled by a dictator is known as a dictatorship.

Fascism- is a form of radical authoritarian nationalism that came to prominence in the early twentieth century in Europe. Fascism is led by a totalitarian single party state with a dictator as its leader. Fascism is often described as being on the far right of the political spectrum.

Great Depression – Severe worldwide economic depression in the 1930s, Economic historians note the start as a result of the collapse of the U.S. stock market on October 29, 1929 known as Black Tuesday.

Hitler Youth/NAZI Youth Movement – Youth organization started in Germany 1922. It was the sole official youth organization in Germany until 1945. It was established with the prime purpose of educating Germany's youth to become ideal NAZI party members as adults. It indoctrinated the youthful members in racism and ideology that would allow them to be total faithful to the Party, Hitler and Germany. They were to become the future Master Race Supermen.

Isolationism – a category of foreign policies institutionalized by leaders who asserted that their nation's best interests were served by keeping other nations issues at a distance. Most Isolationists believe that limiting their country's involvement in other countries' affairs will keep them from being drawn into dangerous and otherwise undesirable conflicts.

Munich Agreement – A settlement permitting NAZI Germany's annexation of certain portions of Czechoslovakia along the country's borders main inhabited by German speakers, for which a new territorial designation known as the Sudetenland was coined. The conference held in Munich was meant to appease Hitler and to hopefully prevent him from taking over more countries. Czechoslovakia was not allowed to attend the conference and have a voice deciding its own fate. The European powers consisting of Germany, France, United Kingdom and Italy signed the agreement giving Hitler the right to have the Sudetenland become a part of Germany.

NAZI Party – The National Socialist German Worker's Party which was active from 1920 to 1945. It originally combined the right wing ideology of nationalism and left wing ideology of socialism. As Hitler and the Third Reich came into power, racism became the central theme of the NAZI Party. The Party strove to develop a "Master Race" by destroying any ethnic or undesirable group that would prevent the reaching of their goal.

Propaganda - a form of communication used to influence the attitude of a population toward some cause or position.

Protective Echelon (SS) – Black uniformed elite corps and self-described "political soldier" of the NAZI Party. This group was founded by Hitler in 1925, as a small group of personal body guards. As the NAZI Party grew so did the SS in power and numbers. It became the most feared group in NAZI Germany.

Regime – refers to a government, especially an oppressive and an undemocratic one.

Reichstag – German governing body/parliament.

Treaty of Versailles - Officially ended World War I. It was signed on June 28, 1919. The most important provision of the treaty was that it made Germany and its allies take total responsibility for World War I. This provision later became known as 'the War Guilt clause." This clause would be responsible in aiding Hitler's rallying call when asking Germany to unite against the harsh punishment dealt Germany after World War I.

Typhus – a disease also known as "camp fever." It is characterized by high fever, headache, rash, stupor, delirium and death. This disease was a common cause of death for prisoners in concentration and POW camps. It is caused by unsanitary conditions and is often contracted by bites and infestation of human body lice. It is treated with antibiotics.

BIBLIOGRAPHY

The Big Book of World War II, Wagner, Melissa, Running Press Classics

The World War I Soldier at Chateau Thierry, Sanford, William R and Carl Green, Capstone Press 1991

The Good Fight: How World War II Was Won, Ambrose, Stephen E., Atheneum Books for Young Readers, 2001, Text by Ambrose Tubbs Inc.